100
NURSERY
RHYMES

HAMLYN
London · New York · Sydney · Toronto

Illustrators:

Glynnis Ambrus   David Anstey   Shirley Bellwood   Bob Geary
Douglas Hall   Lisa Jensen   Susie Lacome   Annabel Large   Tony Morris
John Patience   Peter Richardson   Nancy Stephens   Shirley Tourret

Cover illustration by Peter Richardson

Published 1980 by The Hamlyn Publishing Group Limited
London · New York · Sydney · Toronto
Astronaut House, Feltham, Middlesex, England
© Copyright The Hamlyn Publishing Group Limited 1980

ISBN 0 600 36462 3   Printed in Italy

Contents

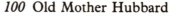

Little Boy Blue

Little Boy Blue
Come blow up your horn!
The sheep's in the meadow,
The cow's in the corn!

Where is the boy
Who looks after the sheep?
He's under the haystack
Fast asleep!

Will you wake him?
No, not I,
For if I do,
He's sure to cry.

There was a little girl

There was a little girl
And she had a little curl,
Right in the middle of her forehead.

When she was good,
She was very, very good,
But when she was bad, she was horrid!

Six little mice

Six little mice sat down to spin;
Pussy passed by and she peeped in.
'What are you doing, my little men?'
'Weaving coats for gentlemen.'
'Shall I come in and cut off your threads?'
'Oh no, Mistress Pussy, you'd bite off our heads!'

The north wind

The north wind doth blow,
   And we shall have snow,
And what will poor robin do then,
   Poor thing?

He'll sit in the barn,
   And keep himself warm,
And hide his head under his wing,
   Poor thing!

The north wind doth blow,
   And we shall have snow,
And what will the swallow do then,
   Poor thing?

12

Oh, do you not know,
   That he's off long ago,
To a country where he will find spring,
   Poor thing!

The north wind doth blow,
   And we shall have snow,
And what will the dormouse do then,
   Poor thing?

Rolled up like a ball,
   In his nest snug and small,
He'll sleep till warm weather comes in,
   Poor thing!

The north wind doth blow,
   And we shall have snow,
And what will the honey-bee do then,
   Poor thing?

In his hive he will stay,
   Till the cold is away,
And then he'll come out in the spring,
   Poor thing!

The north wind doth blow,
   And we shall have snow,
And what will the children do then,
   Poor things?

When lessons are done,
   They must skip, jump and run,
Until they have made themselves warm,
   Poor things!

There was a crooked man

There was a crooked man,
And he walked a crooked mile,
And he found a crooked sixpence,
Beside a crooked style.

He bought a crooked cat,
Which caught a crooked mouse,
And they all lived together
In a crooked little house.

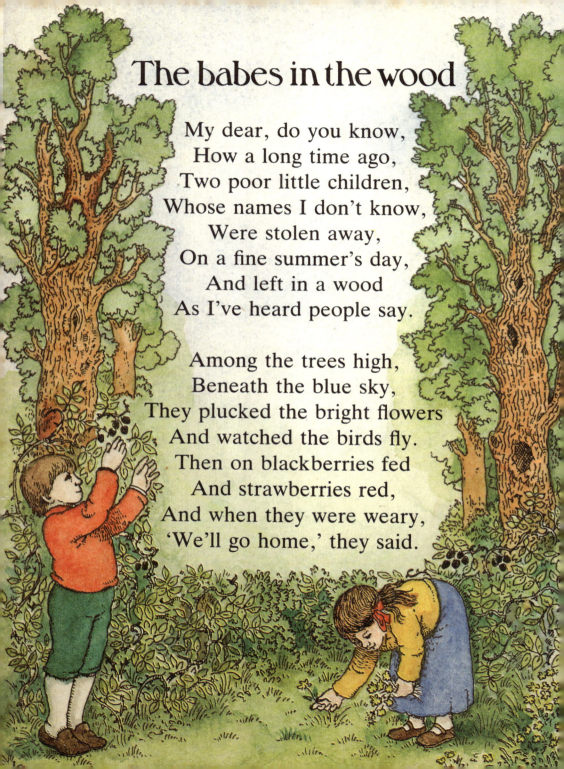

The babes in the wood

My dear, do you know,
How a long time ago,
Two poor little children,
Whose names I don't know,
Were stolen away,
On a fine summer's day,
And left in a wood
As I've heard people say.

Among the trees high,
Beneath the blue sky,
They plucked the bright flowers
And watched the birds fly.
Then on blackberries fed
And strawberries red,
And when they were weary,
'We'll go home,' they said.

But then it was night
And sad was their plight.
The sun it went down
And the moon gave no light.
They sobbed and they sighed,
And they bitterly cried,
And long before morning
They lay down and died.

And when they were dead,
The robins so red,
Brought strawberry leaves
And over them spread.
And all the day long,
The green branches among,
They'd prettily whistle
And this was their song –
'Poor babes in the wood,
Sweet babes in the wood,
Oh, the sad fate of
The babes in the wood.'

I have four sisters

I have four sisters beyond the sea,
    Perry, merry, dixie, dominie.
And they each sent a present to me,
    Perry, merry, dixie, dominie.

The first sent a chicken without e'er a bone,
    Perry, merry, dixie, dominie.
The second a cherry without e'er a stone,
    Perry, merry, dixie, dominie.

The third sent a book which no man could read,
    Perry, merry, dixie, dominie.
The fourth sent a blanket, without e'er a thread,
    Perry, merry, dixie, dominie.

Can there be a chicken without e'er a bone?
    Perry, merry, dixie, dominie.
Can there be a cherry without any stone?
    Perry, merry, dixie, dominie.

Can there be a book which cannot be read?
   Perry, merry, dixie, dominie.
Can there be a blanket without e'er a thread?
   Perry, merry, dixie, dominie.

When the chicken's in the egg there is no bone,
   Perry, merry, dixie, dominie.
When the cherry's in the bud there is no stone,
   Perry, merry, dixie, dominie.

When the book's in the press it cannot be read,
   Perry, merry, dixie, dominie.
When the blanket's in the fleece there is no thread,
   Perry, merry, dixie, dominie.

I wish...

Star light, star bright,
    First star I see tonight,
I wish I may, I wish I might,
    Have the wish, I wish tonight.

Doctor Foster

Doctor Foster went to Gloucester
In a shower of rain.
He stepped in a puddle,
Right up to his middle,
And never went there again!

The muffin man

Have you seen the muffin man?
  The muffin man, the muffin man.
Oh, have you seen the muffin man,
  Who lives down Drury Lane?

Oh yes, I've seen the muffin man,
  The muffin man, the muffin man.
Oh yes, I've seen the muffin man,
  Who lives down Drury Lane.

The farmer's in his den

The farmer's in his den,
  The farmer's in his den,
E-I-E-I,
  The farmer's in his den.

The farmer wants a wife,
  The farmer wants a wife,
E-I-E-I,
  The farmer wants a wife.

The wife wants a child,
  The wife wants a child,
E-I-E-I,
  The wife wants a child.

The child wants a nurse,
  The child wants a nurse,
E-I-E-I,
  The child wants a nurse.

The nurse wants a dog,
  The nurse wants a dog,
E-I-E-I,
  The nurse wants a dog.

We all pat the dog,
  We all pat the dog,
E-I-E-I,
  We all pat the dog.

25

As I was going to Derby

As I was going to Derby,
Upon a market day,
I met the finest sheep, sir,
That ever was fed on hay.

This sheep was fat behind, sir,
This sheep was fat before,
This sheep was ten yards high, sir,
Indeed he could have been more!

The wool upon his back, sir,
Reached up into the sky,
The eagles built their nests there,
For I heard the young ones cry.

This sheep had four legs to walk upon,
This sheep had four legs to stand,
And every leg he had, sir,
Stood on an acre of land.

Now the man who fed the sheep, sir,
He fed him twice a day,
And each time he fed him, sir,
He ate a rick of hay.

O soldier, soldier

'O soldier, soldier, will you marry me,
  With your musket, fife and drum?'
'Oh no, sweet maid, I cannot marry you,
  For I have no coat to put on.'

So off she went to the tailor's shop,
  As fast as legs could run,
And bought him a coat of the very, very best,
  And the soldier put it on.

'O soldier, soldier, will you marry me,
   With your musket, fife and drum?'
'Oh no, sweet maid, I cannot marry you,
   For I have no shoes to put on.'

So off she went to the cobbler's shop,
   As fast as legs could run,
And bought a pair of the very, very best,
   And the soldier put them on.

'O soldier, soldier, will you marry me,
    With your musket, fife and drum?'
'Oh no, sweet maid, I cannot marry you,
    For I have no socks to put on.'

So off she went to the sock-maker's shop,
    As fast as legs could run,
And bought him a pair of the very, very best,
    And the soldier put them on.

'O soldier, soldier, will you marry me,
    With your musket, fife and drum?'
'Oh no, sweet maid, I cannot marry you,
    For I have no hat to put on.'

So off she went to the hatter's shop,
    As fast as legs could run,
And bought him a hat of the very, very best,
    And the soldier put it on.

'O soldier, soldier, will you marry me,
    With your musket, fife and drum?'
'Oh no, sweet maid, I cannot marry you,
    For I have a wife at home!'

There was a piper

There was a piper had a cow
And had no hay to give her.
He played a tune upon his pipes,
'Consider, old cow, consider!'

The old cow considered well
And promised her master money,
Only to play that other tune,
'Corn-riggs are bonny.'

Polly, put the kettle on

Polly, put the kettle on,
Polly, put the kettle on,
Polly, put the kettle on,
We'll all have tea.

Sally, take it off again,
Sally, take it off again,
Sally, take it off again,
They've all gone away.

Girls and boys

Girls and boys come out to play,
The moon doth shine as bright as day.
Leave your supper and leave your sleep
And join your playfellows in the street.
Come with a whoop, come with a call,
Come with a good will or not at all.
Up the ladder and down the wall,
A penny loaf will serve us all.
You find milk and I'll find flour
And we'll have pudding in half an hour.

There was an old woman

There was an old woman tossed up in a basket,
   Seventeen times as high as the moon.
Where she was going I couldn't but ask it,
   For in her hand she carried a broom.

'Old woman, old woman, old woman,' quoth I,
   'Where are you going to up so high?'
Thus she replied, and this was her answer,
   'To brush all the cobwebs off the sky!'

Travelling

One leg in front of the other,
One leg in front of the other,
  As the little dog travelled
  From London to Dover.
And when he came to a stile,
  Jump! He went over.

Mr. Nobody

I know a funny little man,
As quiet as a mouse.
He does the mischief that is done,
In everybody's house!
Though no one ever sees his face,
Yet one and all agree,
That every plate we break was cracked
By Mr. Nobody.

'Tis he who always tears our books,
Who leaves the door ajar.
He picks the buttons from our shirts,
And scatters pins afar.
That squeaking door will always squeak –
For prithee, don't you see?
We leave the oiling to be done
By Mr. Nobody.

He puts damp wood upon the fire,
So kettles will not boil.
His are the feet that bring in mud
And all the carpets soil.
The papers that are so often lost –
Who had them last but he?
There's no one tosses them about
But Mr. Nobody.

The fingermarks upon the door
By none of us were made.
We never leave the blinds undone,
To let the curtains fade.
The ink we never spill! The boots,
That lying round you see,
Are not our boots – they all belong
To Mr. Nobody.

Wee Willie Winkie

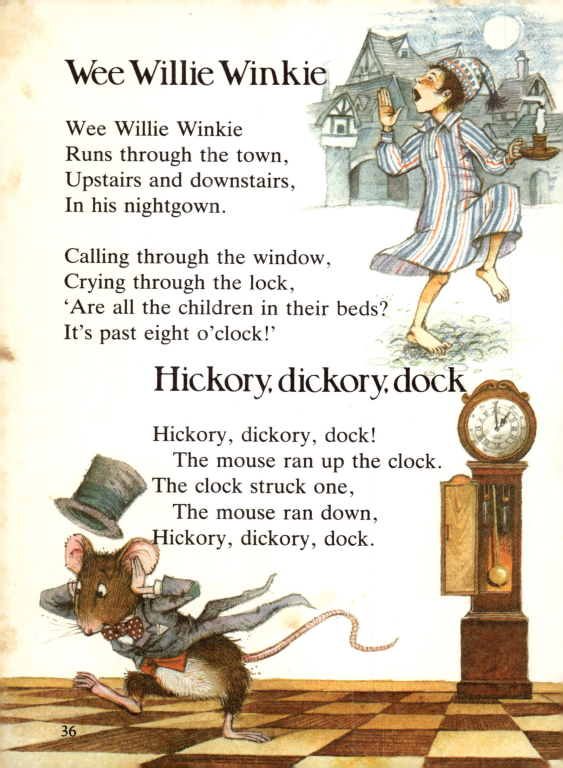

Wee Willie Winkie
Runs through the town,
Upstairs and downstairs,
In his nightgown.

Calling through the window,
Crying through the lock,
'Are all the children in their beds?
It's past eight o'clock!'

Hickory, dickory, dock

Hickory, dickory, dock!
    The mouse ran up the clock.
The clock struck one,
    The mouse ran down,
Hickory, dickory, dock.

Tweedle-dum and Tweedle-dee

Tweedle-dum and Tweedle-dee
Resolved to have a battle.
For Tweedle-dum said Tweedle-dee
Had spoiled his nice new rattle.

Just then flew by a monstrous crow
As big as a tar-barrel,
Which frightened both the heroes so
They quite forgot their quarrel.

Three jolly huntsmen

There were three jolly huntsmen,
  As I have heard men say,
And they would go a-hunting, boys,
  Upon St. David's Day.
And all the day they hunted
  But nothing could they find,
Except a ship a-sailing,
  A-sailing with the wind.

One said it surely was a ship,
　　The second he said, 'Nay.'
The third declared it was a house
　　With the chimney blown away.
Then all night they hunted
　　And nothing could they find,
Except the moon a-gliding,
　　A-gliding with the wind.

One said it surely was the moon,
　　The second he said, 'Nay.'
The third declared it was a cheese
　　With half of it cut away.
Then all next day they hunted
　　And nothing could they find,
Except a hedgehog in a bush,
　　And that they left behind.

One said it was a hedgehog,
   The second he said, 'Nay.'
The third, it was a pincushion,
   With pins stuck in wrong way.
Then all next day they hunted
   And nothing could they find,
Except a hare in a turnip field,
   And that they left behind.

One said it surely was a hare,
   The second he said, 'Nay.'
The third he said it was a calf,
   And the cow had run away.
Then all next day they hunted
   And nothing could they find,
But one owl in a holly-tree,
   And that they left behind.

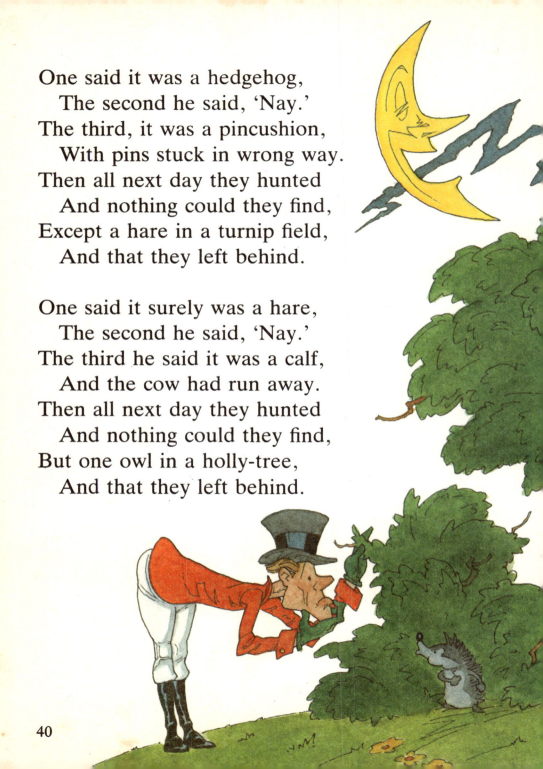

One said it surely was an owl,
　　The second he said, 'Nay.'
The third said 'twas an aged man
　　Whose beard was going grey.
Then all three jolly Welshmen
　　Came riding home at last,
'For three days we have nothing killed,
　　And never broke our fast!'

I had a little nut tree

I had a little nut tree,
Nothing would it bear,
But a silver nutmeg
And a golden pear.
The King of Spain's daughter
Came to visit me,
And all for the sake of my little nut tree!

I skipped over water,
I danced over sea,
And all the birds in the air,
Couldn't catch me!

Down in yonder meadow

Down in yonder meadow where the green
                           grass grows,
  Pretty Polly Petticoat bleaches her clothes.
She sang, she sang, she sang, oh, so sweet,
  She sang, 'Oh, come over,' across the street.

He kissed her, he kissed her, he bought
                           her a gown,
  A gown of rich crimson to wear in the town.
He bought her a gown and a guinea gold ring,
  A guinea, a guinea, a guinea gold ring.

Up street, and down, shine the windows made
                           of glass,
  Oh, isn't Polly Petticoat a pretty young lass?
Cherries in her cheeks, and ringlets in her hair,
  Hear her singing sweetly up and down the stair.

The animals came in two by two

The animals came in two by two,
Hurrah, hurrah.
The centipede with the kangaroo,
Hurrah, hurrah.
And they all went into the ark
For to get out of the rain.

The animals came in three by three,
Hurrah, hurrah.
The elephant on the back of the flea,
Hurrah, hurrah.
And they all went into the ark
For to get out of the rain.

The animals came in four by four,
Hurrah, hurrah.
The camel, he got stuck in the door,
Hurrah, hurrah.
And they all went into the ark
For to get out of the rain.

The animals came in five by five,
Hurrah, hurrah.
The bees made sure to bring their hive,
Hurrah, hurrah.
And they all went into the ark
For to get out of the rain.

The animals came in six by six,
Hurrah, hurrah.
The monkey, he was up to his tricks,
Hurrah, hurrah.
And they all went into the ark
For to get out of the rain.

45

The animals went in seven by seven,
Hurrah, hurrah.
Some went to hell, and some to heaven,
Hurrah, hurrah.
And they all went into the ark
For to get out of the rain.

The animals went in eight by eight,
Hurrah, hurrah.
The worm was early, the bird was late,
Hurrah, hurrah.
And they all went into the ark
For to get out of the rain.

The animals went in nine by nine,
Hurrah, hurrah.
But the unicorn was not in time,
Hurrah, hurrah.
And they all went into the ark
For to get out of the rain.

The animals went in ten by ten,
Hurrah, hurrah.
If you want any more you must sing it again.
Hurrah, hurrah.
And they all went into the ark
For to get out of the rain.

My mother said

My mother said, I never should,
Play with the gipsies in the wood.

If I did then she would say:
'Naughty girl to disobey!'

'Your hair shan't curl and your shoes shan't shine,
You gipsy girl you shan't be mine.'

And my father said that if I did,
He'd rap my head with the tea-pot lid.

My mother said, I never should,
Play with the gipsies in the wood.

The wood was dark, the grass was green,
By came Sally with a tambourine.

I went to sea – no ship to get across,
I paid ten shillings for a blind white horse.

I upped on his back and was off in a crack.
'Sally, tell my mother I shall never come back!'

Ladybird, ladybird

Ladybird, ladybird,
Fly away home.
Your house is on fire,
And your children are gone.
All except one,
Whose name is Anne,
And she crept under
The frying pan!

Blow, wind, blow

Blow, wind, blow,
And go, mill, go!
That the miller may grind his corn,
That the baker may take it,
And into bread make it,
And bring us a loaf in the morn.

One, two, three, four, five

One, two, three, four, five,
Once I caught a fish alive.
Six, seven, eight, nine, ten,
Then I let it go again.

Why did you let it go?
Because it bit my finger so.
Which finger did it bite?
This little finger on the right.

Tom, Tom, the piper's son

Tom, Tom, the piper's son,
Stole a pig and away did run.
The pig was eat, and Tom was beat,
And Tom went crying down the street.

Mary had a little lamb

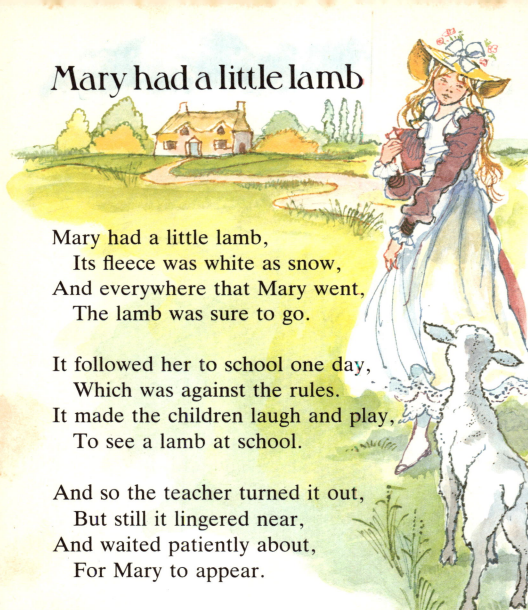

Mary had a little lamb,
   Its fleece was white as snow,
And everywhere that Mary went,
   The lamb was sure to go.

It followed her to school one day,
   Which was against the rules.
It made the children laugh and play,
   To see a lamb at school.

And so the teacher turned it out,
   But still it lingered near,
And waited patiently about,
   For Mary to appear.

'Why does the lamb love Mary so?'
   The eager children cry.
'Why, 'cos Mary loves the lamb, you know,'
   The teacher did reply.

I love little pussy

I love little pussy,
Her coat is so warm,
And if I don't hurt her
She'll do me no harm.

So I'll not pull her tail,
Nor drive her away,
But pussy cat and I
Will sit quietly and play.

She will sit by my side,
And I'll give her some food,
And pussy will love me
Because I am good.

53

Three little kittens

Three little kittens,
They lost their mittens,
And they began to cry,
'O Mother dear,
We sadly fear,
That we have lost our mittens.'

'What! Lost your mittens,
You naughty kittens!
Then you shall have no pie.
Mee-ow, mee-ow,
Then you shall have no pie.'

The three little kittens,
They found their mittens,
And they began to cry,
'O Mother dear,
Come here, come here,
For we have found our mittens!'

'What! Found your mittens,
You good little kittens,
Then you shall have some pie.
Purr, purr, purr, purr,
Then you shall have some pie.'

The three little kittens
Put on their mittens,
And soon ate up their pie.
'O Mother dear, we greatly fear
That we have soiled our mittens.'

'What! Soiled your mittens,
You naughty kittens.'
And they began to cry,
'Mee-ow, mee-ow,'
And they began to cry.

The three little kittens,
They washed their mittens,
And hung them out to dry.
'O Mother dear, come here, come here,
For we have washed our mittens.'

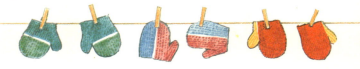

'What! Washed your mittens?
You good little kittens.
Now hush, hush,
I smell a mouse close by,
I smell a mouse close by!'

The man in the moon

The man in the moon,
Came down too soon,
And asked the way to Norwich.
He went by the south,
And burned his mouth,
While eating cold plum porridge!

Two little blue birds

Two little blue birds
    Sitting on a wall.
One named Peter,
    One named Paul.

Fly away, Peter,
    Fly away, Paul.
Come back, Peter,
    Come back, Paul!

Pussy cat, pussy cat

'Pussy cat, pussy cat,
Where have you been?'

'I've been up to London
To visit the Queen.'

'Pussy cat, pussy cat,
What did you there?'

'I frightened a little mouse
Under her chair.'

Woe is me!

Woe is me, woe is me!
The acorn's not yet
Fallen from the tree,
That's to grow the wood,
That's to make the cradle,
That's to rock the bairn,
That'll grow to the man,
Who's to marry me!

Twinkle, twinkle little star

Twinkle, twinkle little star,
How I wonder what you are!
Up above the world so high,
Like a diamond in the sky.

In the dark blue sky you keep,
Watching over while I sleep.
For you never shut your eye,
'Til the sun is in the sky.

And the traveller in the dark,
Thanks you for your tiny spark.
He could not see which way to go,
If you did not twinkle so.

Twinkle, twinkle little star,
How I wonder what you are!
Up above the world so high,
Like a diamond in the sky.

Who killed Cock Robin?

Who killed Cock Robin?
'I,' said the Sparrow,
'With my bow and arrow,
I killed Cock Robin.'

Who saw him die?
'I,' said the Fly,
'With my little eye,
I saw him die.'

Who'll make the shroud?
'I,' said the Beetle,
'With my thread and needle,
I'll make the shroud.'

Who'll dig the grave?
'I,' said the Owl,
'With my pick and shovel,
I'll dig the grave.'

Who'll be the parson?
'I,' said the Rook,
'With my little book,
I'll be the parson.'

Who'll be the clerk?
'I,' said the Lark,
'If it's not in the dark,
I'll be the clerk.'

Who'll be chief mourner?
'I,' said the Dove,
'I mourn for my love,
I'll be chief mourner.'

Who'll carry the coffin?
'I,' said the Kite,
'If it's not through the night,
I'll carry the coffin.'

Who'll bear the pall?
'We,' said the Wrens,
Both the cock and the hen,
'We'll bear the pall.'

Who'll sing a psalm?
'I,' said the Hen,
'I sing now and then,
I'll sing a psalm.'

Who'll toll the bell?
'I,' said the Thrush,
As she sat on a bush,
'I'll toll the bell.'

All the birds of the air
Fell a-sighing and a-sobbing,
When they heard the bell toll
For poor Cock Robin.

Pat-a-cake, pat-a-cake

Pat-a-cake, pat-a-cake,
Baker's man.
Bake me a cake
As fast as you can.
Prick it and nick it
And mark it with 'B',
And put it in the oven
For Baby and me.

As I was going to St. Ives

As I was going to St. Ives,
I met a man with seven wives.
Each wife had seven sacks.
Each sack had seven cats.
Each cat had seven kits.
Kits, cats, sacks and wives,
How many were going to St. Ives?

The Queen of Hearts

The Queen of Hearts,
   She made some tarts,
All on a summer's day.
   The Knave of Hearts,
He stole the tarts,
   And took them clean away.

The King of Hearts,
   Called for the tarts,
And beat the Knave full sore.
   The Knave of Hearts
Brought back the tarts,
   And vowed he'd steal no more.

Hey diddle-diddle

Hey diddle-diddle,
    The cat and the fiddle,
The cow jumped over the moon.
    The little boy laughed
To see such fun,
    And the dish ran away with the spoon!

66

This is the way

This is the way the ladies ride,
  Clip-clop, clip-clop, clip-clop.
This is the way the ladies ride,
  Clip-clop, clip-clop, clip-clop.

This is the way the gentlemen ride,
  Gall-op, gall-op, gall-op.
This is the way the gentlemen ride,
  Gall-op, gall-op, gall-op.

This is the way the farmers ride,
  Hobbledy-hoy, hobbledy-hoy, hobbledy-hoy.
This is the way the farmers ride,
  Hobbledy-hoy, hobbledy-hoy, hobbledy-hoy.

A fox went out

A fox went out one frosty night
And he begged of the moon to give him light,
For he had many miles to go that night
Before he reached his den O!
Den O! Den O!
For he'd many miles to go that night
Before he reached his den O!

The first place he went was the farmer's yard,
Where the ducks and the geese declared it hard
That their nerves should be shaken
   and their rest so marred,
By a visit from Mr Fox O!
Fox O! Fox O!
That their nerves should be shaken
   and their rest so marred,
By a visit from Mr Fox O!

He took the grey goose by the neck,
And swung him right across his back.
The grey goose cried, 'Quack-quack,
   quack-quack,'
With his legs all dangling down O!
Down O! Down O!
The grey goose cried, 'Quack-quack,
   quack-quack,'
With his legs all dangling down O!

Old Mother Slipper-Slopper jumped out of bed
And out of the window she popped her head.
'O John, John, the grey goose is gone,
And the fox is off to his den O!'
Den O! Den O!
'O John, John, the grey goose is gone
And the fox is off to his den O!'

John ran up to the top of the hill,
And he blew his whistle loud and shrill.
Said the fox, 'That's very pretty music, still,
I'd rather be in my den O!'
Den O! Den O!
Said the fox, 'That's very pretty music, still,
I'd rather be in my den O!'

70

The fox went back to his hungry den,
And his dear little foxes, eight, nine, ten.
Said they, 'Good Daddy, you must go there again,
For it must be a mighty fine town O!'
Town O! Town O!
Said they, 'O Daddy, you must go there again,
For it must be a mighty fine town O!'

The fox and his wife without any strife
Said they never ate a better goose in their life.
They did very well without fork or knife
And the little ones picked on the bones O!
Bones O! Bones O!
They did very well without fork or knife
And the little ones picked on the bones O!

I had a cat

I had a cat and the cat pleased me,
I fed my cat by yonder tree:
Cat goes, 'Mee-ow, mee-ow.'

I had a hen and the hen pleased me,
I fed my hen by yonder tree:
Hen goes, 'Cluck, cluck,'
Cat goes, 'Mee-ow, mee-ow.'

I had a duck and the duck pleased me,
I fed my duck by yonder tree:
Duck goes, 'Quack, quack,'
Hen goes, 'Cluck, cluck,'
Cat goes, 'Mee-ow, mee-ow.'

I had a sheep and the sheep pleased me,
I fed my sheep by yonder tree:
Sheep goes, 'Baa, baa,'
Duck goes, 'Quack, quack,'
Hen goes, 'Cluck, cluck,'
Cat goes, 'Mee-ow, mee-ow.'

I had a pig and the pig pleased me,
I fed my pig by yonder tree:
Pig goes, 'Grunt, grunt,'
Sheep goes, 'Baa, baa,'
Duck goes, 'Quack, quack,'
Hen goes, 'Cluck, cluck,'
Cat goes, 'Mee-ow, mee-ow.'

I had a cow and the cow pleased me,
I fed my cow by yonder tree:
Cow goes, 'Moo, moo,'
Pig goes, 'Grunt, grunt,'
Sheep goes, 'Baa, baa,'
Duck goes, 'Quack, quack,'
Hen goes, 'Cluck, cluck,'
Cat goes, 'Mee-ow, mee-ow.'

I had a horse and the horse pleased me,
I fed my horse by yonder tree:
Horse goes, 'Neigh, neigh,'
Cow goes, 'Moo, moo,'
Pig goes, 'Grunt, grunt,'
Sheep goes, 'Baa baa,'
Duck goes, 'Quack, quack,'
Hen goes, 'Cluck, cluck,'
Cat goes, 'Mee-ow, mee-ow.'

I had a dog and the dog pleased me,
I fed my dog by yonder tree:
Dog goes, 'Ruff, ruff,'
Horse goes, 'Neigh, neigh,'
Cow goes, 'Moo, moo,'
Pig goes, 'Grunt, grunt,'
Sheep goes, 'Baa, baa,'
Duck goes, 'Quack, quack,'
Hen goes, 'Cluck, cluck,'
Cat goes, 'Mee-ow, mee-ow.'

I saw three ships

I saw three ships come sailing by,
    Come sailing by, come sailing by.
I saw three ships come sailing by,
    On New Year's Day in the morning.

And what do you think was in them then,
    Was in them then, was in them then?
And what do you think was in them then,
    On New Year's Day in the morning?

Three pretty girls were in them then,
    Were in them then, were in them then.
Three pretty girls were in them then,
    On New Year's Day in the morning.

One could whistle and one could sing,
    And one could play on the violin.
Such joy there was at their coming,
    On New Year's Day in the morning.

Good King Arthur

When good King Arthur ruled this land,
He was a goodly King.
He stole three pecks of barley meal
To make a bag-pudding.

A bag-pudding the King did make,
And stuffed it well with plums,
And in it put great lumps of fat
As big as my two thumbs.

The King and Queen did eat thereof
And noblemen beside.
And what they could not eat that night,
The Queen next morning fried!

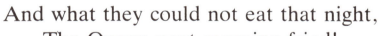

Here we go round the mulberry bush

Here we go round the mulberry bush,
The mulberry bush, the mulberry bush.
Here we go round the mulberry bush,
On a cold and frosty morning.

This is the way we wash our face,
Wash our face, wash our face.
This is the way we wash our face,
On a cold and frosty morning.

This is the way we clean our teeth,
Clean our teeth, clean our teeth.
This is the way we clean our teeth,
On a cold and frosty morning.

This is the way we go to school,
Go to school, go to school.
This is the way we go to school,
On a cold and frosty morning.

This is the way we do our lessons,
Do our lessons, do our lessons.
This is the way we do our lessons,
On a cold and frosty morning.

This is the way we go out to play,
Out to play, out to play.
This is the way we go out to play,
On a cold and frosty morning.

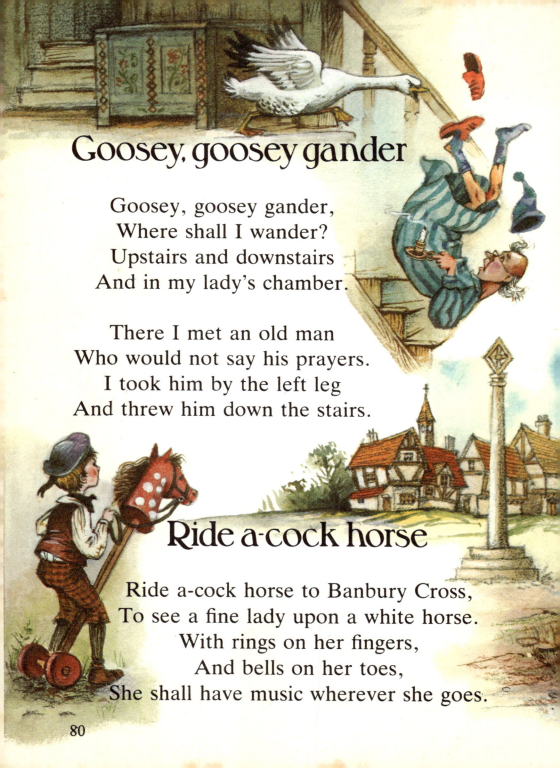

Goosey, goosey gander

Goosey, goosey gander,
Where shall I wander?
Upstairs and downstairs
And in my lady's chamber.

There I met an old man
Who would not say his prayers.
I took him by the left leg
And threw him down the stairs.

Ride a-cock horse

Ride a-cock horse to Banbury Cross,
To see a fine lady upon a white horse.
With rings on her fingers,
And bells on her toes,
She shall have music wherever she goes.

Simple Simon

Simple Simon met a pieman
   Going to the fair.
Said Simple Simon to the pieman,
   'Please let me taste your ware.'

Said the pieman to Simple Simon,
   'Show me first your penny.'
Said Simple Simon to the pieman,
   'Indeed I have not any.'

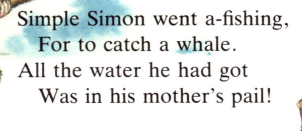

Simple Simon went a-fishing,
   For to catch a whale.
All the water he had got
   Was in his mother's pail!

Simple Simon went to look
   If plums grew on a thistle.
He pricked his finger very much,
   Which made poor Simon whistle!

The twelve days of Christmas

On the first day of Christmas
My true love sent to me:
A partridge in a pear tree.

On the second day of Christmas
My true love sent to me:
Two turtle doves,
And a partridge in a pear tree.

On the third day of Christmas
My true love sent to me:
Three French hens,
Two turtle doves,
And a partridge in a pear tree.

On the fourth day of Christmas,
My true love sent to me:
Four colly birds,
Three French hens,
Two turtle doves,
And a partridge in a pear tree.

On the fifth day of Christmas
My true love sent to me:
Five gold rings,
Four colly birds,
Three French hens,
Two turtle doves,
And a partridge in a pear tree.

On the sixth day of Christmas
My true love sent to me:
Six geese a-laying,
Five gold rings,
Four colly birds,
Three French hens,
Two turtle doves,
And a partridge in a pear tree.

On the seventh day of Christmas
My true love sent to me:
Seven swans a-swimming,
Six geese a-laying,
Five gold rings,
Four colly birds,
Three French hens,
Two turtle doves,
And a partridge in a pear tree.

On the eighth day of Christmas
My true love sent to me:
Eight maids a-milking,
Seven swans a-swimming,
Six geese a-laying,
Five gold rings,
Four colly birds,
Three French hens,
Two turtle doves,
And a partridge in a pear tree.

On the ninth day of Christmas
My true love sent to me:
Nine drummers drumming,
Eight maids a-milking,
Seven swans a-swimming,
Six geese a-laying,
Five gold rings,
Four colly birds,
Three French hens,
Two turtle doves,
And a partridge in a pear tree.

On the tenth day of Christmas
My true love sent to me:
Ten pipers piping,
Nine drummers drumming,
Eight maids a-milking,
Seven swans a-swimming,
Six geese a-laying,
Five gold rings,
Four colly birds,
Three French hens,
Two turtle doves,
And a partridge in a pear tree.

On the eleventh day of Christmas
My true love sent to me:
Eleven ladies dancing,
Ten pipers piping,
Nine drummers drumming,
Eight maids a-milking,
Seven swans a-swimming,
Six geese a-laying,
Five gold rings,
Four colly birds,
Three French hens,
Two turtle doves,
And a partridge in a pear tree.

On the twelfth day of Christmas
My true love sent to me:
Twelve lords a-leaping,
Eleven ladies dancing,
Ten pipers piping,
Nine drummers drumming,
Eight maids a-milking,
Seven swans a-swimming,
Six geese a-laying,
Five gold rings,
Four colly birds,
Three French hens,
Two turtle doves,
And a partridge in a pear tree.

It's raining!

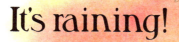

It's raining, it's pouring,
  The old man's snoring.
He went to bed,
  And bumped his head,
And couldn't get up
  In the morning.

The lion and the unicorn

The lion and the unicorn
Were fighting for the crown.
The lion beat the unicorn
  All around the town.

Some gave them white bread,
And some gave them brown,
And some gave them plum cake,
And drummed them out of town.

January brings the snow

January brings the snow,
Makes our feet and fingers glow.

February brings the rain,
Thaws the frozen lake again.

March brings breezes loud and shrill,
Stirs the dancing daffodil.

April brings the primrose sweet,
Scatters daisies at our feet.

May brings flocks of pretty lambs,
Skipping by their fleecy dams.

June brings tulips, lilies, roses,
Fills the children's hands with posies.

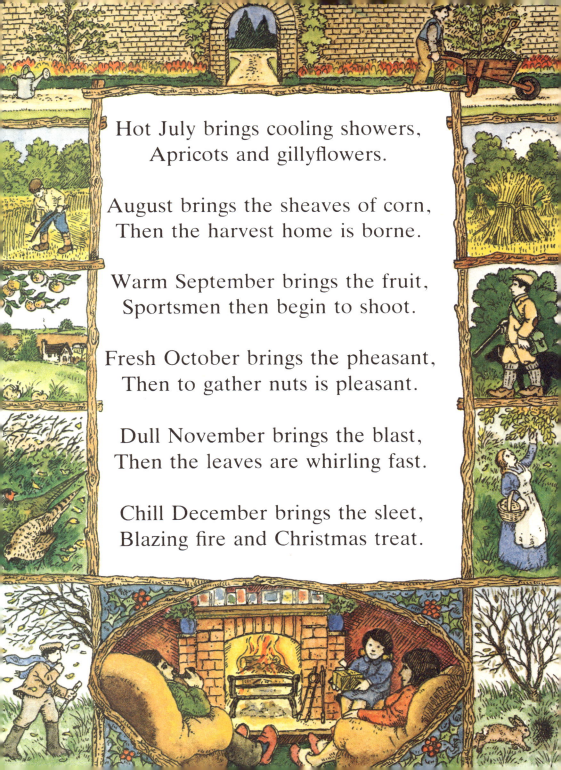

Hot July brings cooling showers,
Apricots and gillyflowers.

August brings the sheaves of corn,
Then the harvest home is borne.

Warm September brings the fruit,
Sportsmen then begin to shoot.

Fresh October brings the pheasant,
Then to gather nuts is pleasant.

Dull November brings the blast,
Then the leaves are whirling fast.

Chill December brings the sleet,
Blazing fire and Christmas treat.

Sing a song of sixpence

Sing a song of sixpence,
A pocket full of rye.
Four and twenty blackbirds,
Baked in a pie!

When the pie was opened,
The birds began to sing.
Wasn't that a dainty dish,
To set before the king?

The king was in his counting house,
Counting out his money.
The queen was in the parlour,
Eating bread and honey.

The maid was in the garden,
Hanging out the clothes,
When down came a blackbird
And pecked off her nose!

Three blind mice

Three blind mice, three blind mice,
See how they run, see how they run.
They all ran after the farmer's wife,
Who cut off their tales with a carving knife.
Did you ever see such a thing in your life
As three blind mice?

I had a little pony

I had a little pony,
His name was Dapple Grey.
I lent him to a lady,
To ride a mile away.

She whipped him, she lashed him,
She rode him through the mire.
I would not lend my pony now,
For all the lady's hire.

Jack and Jill

Jack and Jill went up the hill
  To fetch a pail of water.
Jack fell down and broke his crown
  And Jill came tumbling after.

Up Jack got and home did trot
  As fast as he could caper.
He went to bed and wrapped his head
  In vinegar and brown paper.

Aiken Drum

There was a man lived in the moon,
   Lived in the moon, lived in the moon.
There was a man lived in the moon,
   And his name was Aiken Drum.

And he played upon a ladle,
   A ladle, a ladle.
And he played upon a ladle,
   And his name was Aiken Drum.

And his hat was made of good cream cheese,
   Good cream cheese, good cream cheese.
And his hat was made of good cream cheese,
   And his name was Aiken Drum.

And his coat was made of good roast beef,
   Good roast beef, good roast beef.
And his coat was made of good roast beef,
   And his name was Aiken Drum.

And his buttons were made of penny loaves,
  Penny loaves, penny loaves.
And his buttons were made of penny loaves,
  And his name was Aiken Drum.

And his waistcoat was made of a pastry crust,
  A pastry crust, a pastry crust.
And his waistcoat was made of a pastry crust,
  And his name was Aiken Drum.

There was a man lived in the moon,
  Lived in the moon, lived in the moon.
There was a man lived in the moon,
  And his name was Aiken Drum.

The robin and the wren

The robin and the redbreast,
The robin and the wren,
If you take them out of their nest
You'll never thrive again.

The robin and the redbreast,
The martin and the swallow,
If you touch one of their eggs
Ill luck is sure to follow.

The grand old Duke of York

The grand old Duke of York,
He had ten thousand men.
He marched them up to the top of the hill,
And he marched them down again.

And when they were up, they were up,
And when they were down, they were down,
And when they were only half-way up,
They were neither up nor down.

Hot cross buns!

Hot cross buns,
   Hot cross buns,
One a penny,
   Two a penny,
Hot cross buns!

If you haven't any daughters
   Give them to your sons,
One a penny,
   Two a penny,
Hot cross buns!

Old Mother Hubbard

Old Mother Hubbard,
　She went to the cupboard,
To fetch her poor dog a bone.
　But when she got there,
The cupboard was bare,
　And so the poor dog had none.

She went to the grocer's
　To buy him some tea,
But when she got back,
　He was climbing a tree.

She went to the hatter's
　To buy him a hat,
But when she got back,
　He was chasing the cat.

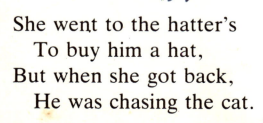

She went to the tailor's
  To buy him a coat,
But when she got back,
  He was milking the goat.

She went to the butcher's
  To buy him some meat,
And at last the poor dog
  Got something to eat!

The dame made a curtsey,
  The dog made a bow.
The dame said, 'Your servant,'
  The dog said, 'Bow-wow.'

London Bridge is falling down

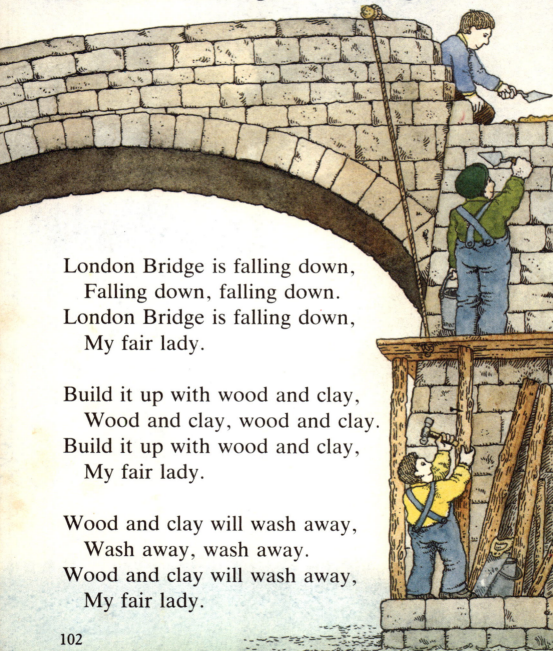

London Bridge is falling down,
Falling down, falling down.
London Bridge is falling down,
My fair lady.

Build it up with wood and clay,
Wood and clay, wood and clay.
Build it up with wood and clay,
My fair lady.

Wood and clay will wash away,
Wash away, wash away.
Wood and clay will wash away,
My fair lady.

Build it up with bricks and mortar,
  Bricks and mortar, bricks and mortar.
Build it up with bricks and mortar,
  My fair lady.

Bricks and mortar will not stay,
  Will not stay, will not stay.
Bricks and mortar will not stay,
  My fair lady.

Build it up with iron and steel,
  Iron and steel, iron and steel.
Build it up with iron and steel,
  My fair lady.

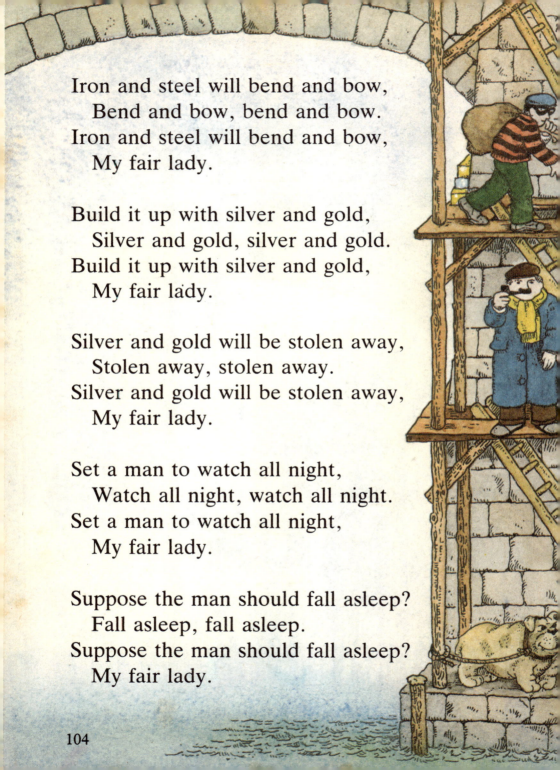

Iron and steel will bend and bow,
   Bend and bow, bend and bow.
Iron and steel will bend and bow,
   My fair lady.

Build it up with silver and gold,
   Silver and gold, silver and gold.
Build it up with silver and gold,
   My fair lady.

Silver and gold will be stolen away,
   Stolen away, stolen away.
Silver and gold will be stolen away,
   My fair lady.

Set a man to watch all night,
   Watch all night, watch all night.
Set a man to watch all night,
   My fair lady.

Suppose the man should fall asleep?
   Fall asleep, fall asleep.
Suppose the man should fall asleep?
   My fair lady.

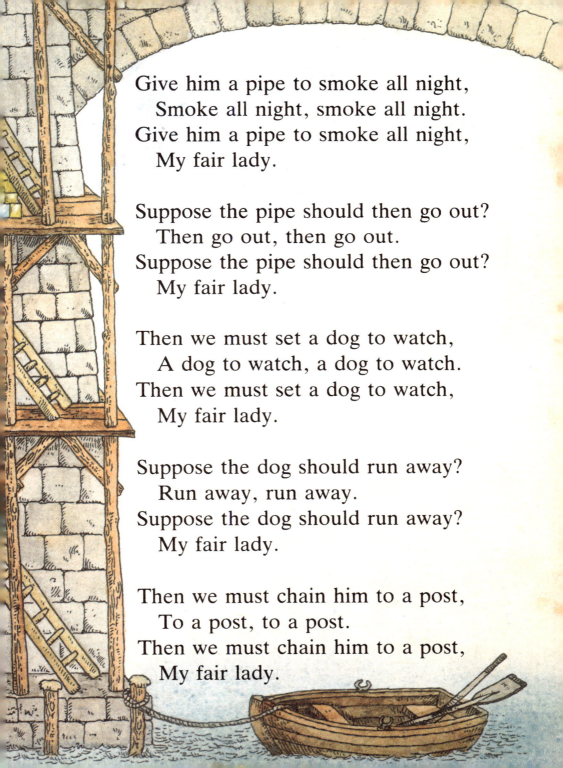

Give him a pipe to smoke all night,
  Smoke all night, smoke all night.
Give him a pipe to smoke all night,
  My fair lady.

Suppose the pipe should then go out?
  Then go out, then go out.
Suppose the pipe should then go out?
  My fair lady.

Then we must set a dog to watch,
  A dog to watch, a dog to watch.
Then we must set a dog to watch,
  My fair lady.

Suppose the dog should run away?
  Run away, run away.
Suppose the dog should run away?
  My fair lady.

Then we must chain him to a post,
  To a post, to a post.
Then we must chain him to a post,
  My fair lady.

There was a little woman

There was a little woman,
As I have heard tell,
She went to market
Her eggs for to sell.
She went to market
All on a market day,
And she fell asleep
On the king's highway.

There came by a pedlar,
Whose name was Stout,
And he cut her petticoats
All round about.
He cut her petticoats
Up to her knees,
Which made the poor woman
To shiver and sneeze.

When this little woman
Began to awake,
She began to shiver
And she began to shake.
She began to shake
And she began to cry,
'God have mercy on me
This is none of I!'

'But if this be I,
As I do hope it be,
I have a little dog at home
And he knows me.
If it be I
He'll wag his little tail,
And if it be not I
He'll bark and loudly wail.'

107

Home went the little woman
All in the dark,
Up starts the little dog
And he began to bark.
He began to bark
And she began to cry,
'God have mercy on me
This is none of I!'

108

Baa, baa, black sheep

Baa, baa, black sheep,
Have you any wool?

Yes Sir, yes Sir,
Three bags full.

One for my master,
And one for my dame.

And one for the little boy
Who lives down the lane.

Lavender's blue

Lavender's blue, dilly, dilly,
   Lavender's green.
When I am King, dilly, dilly,
   You shall be Queen.

Call up your men, dilly, dilly,
   And set them to work.
Some shall cut corn, dilly, dilly,
   And some pull the cart.

Some shall make hay, dilly, dilly,
   Some shall thresh corn.
While you and I, dilly, dilly,
   Keep ourselves warm.

Little diamonds

A million little diamonds
Twinkled on the trees,
And all the little maidens said,
'A jewel, if you please!'

But while they held their hands outstretched,
To catch the diamonds gay,
A million little sunbeams came
And stole them all away!

This little pig

This little pig went to market,
This little pig stayed at home,
This little pig had roast beef,
But this little pig had none.
And this little pig cried,
'Wee, wee, wee,
I can't find my way home!'

How many miles?

How many miles to Babylon?
Threescore miles and ten.

Can I get there by candlelight?
Yes, and back again.

If your heels are nimble and light,
You will get there by candlelight.

Higgledy, piggledy

Higgledy, piggledy, my black hen,
She lays eggs for gentlemen.
Gentlemen come every day
To see what my black hen doth lay.
Sometimes nine and sometimes ten,
Higgledy, piggledy, my black hen.

A farmer went trotting

A farmer went trotting upon his grey mare,
  Bumpety, bumpety, bump,
With his daughter behind him so rosy and fair,
  Lumpety, lumpety, lump.

A raven cried, 'Croak!' and they
          all tumbled down,
  Bumpety, bumpety, bump.
The mare broke her knees and
          the farmer his crown,
  Lumpety, lumpety, lump.

The mischievous raven flew laughing away,
  Bumpety, bumpety, bump,
And vowed he would do it again the next day,
  Lumpety, lumpety, lump!

Where are you going?

'Where are you going to, my pretty maid?'
    'I'm going a-milking, Sir,' she said,
'Sir,' she said, 'Sir,' she said.
    'I'm going a-milking, Sir,' she said.

'May I go with you, my pretty maid?'
    'You're kindly welcome, Sir,' she said,
'Sir,' she said, 'Sir,' she said.
    'You're kindly welcome, Sir,' she said.

'What is your father, my pretty maid?'
    'My father's a farmer, Sir,' she said,
'Sir,' she said, 'Sir,' she said.
    'My father's a farmer, Sir,' she said.

'What is your fortune, my pretty maid?'
    'My face is my fortune, Sir,' she said,
'Sir,' she said, 'Sir,' she said.
    'My face is my fortune, Sir,' she said.

'Then I can't marry you, my pretty maid.'
    'Nobody asked you, Sir,' she said.
'Sir,' she said, 'Sir,' she said.
    'Nobody asked you, Sir,' she said.

Betty Botter

Betty Botter bought some butter,
  'But,' she said, 'the butter's bitter!
If I put it in my batter,
  It will make my batter bitter.
But a bit of better butter
  Will make my batter better!'

So she bought a bit of butter,
  Better than the bitter butter.
And she put it in her batter,
  And the batter was not bitter.
So 'twas better Betty Botter
  Bought some better butter.

Little Tommy Tucker

Little Tommy Tucker
Sang for his supper.
What shall we give him?
Brown bread and butter.
How will he cut it
Without a knife?
How can he marry
Without e'er a wife?

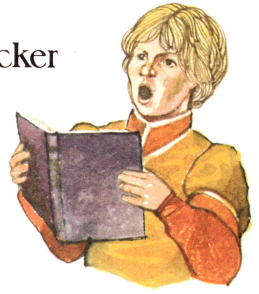

Humpty Dumpty

Humpty Dumpty sat on the wall,
Humpty Dumpty had a great fall.
All the king's horses and all the king's men,
Couldn't put Humpty together again!

The months

Thirty days hath September,
April, June and November.
All the rest have thirty-one,
Excepting February alone,
And that has twenty-eight days clear,
And twenty-nine in each leap year.

Hush-a-bye baby

Hush-a-bye baby,
On the tree top.
When the wind blows,
The cradle will rock.
When the bough bends
The cradle will fall,
And down will come baby,
Cradle and all.

Ding dong bell

Ding dong bell,
   Pussy's in the well.
Who put her in?
   Little Johnny Green.
Who pulled her out?
   Little Tommy Stout.

What a naughty boy was that
   To try and drown poor pussy cat,
Who never did any harm,
   But killed all the mice
In his father's barn.

Are you going to Scarborough Fair?

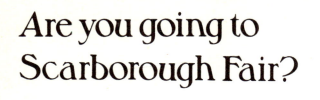

Are you going to Scarborough Fair?
  Parsley, sage, rosemary and thyme.
Remember me to one who lives there,
  She once was a true love of mine.

Ask her to make me a cambric shirt,
  Parsley, sage, rosemary and thyme,
Without any seam or needlework,
  For she once was a true love of mine.

120

Ask her to wash it in yonder well,
  Parsley, sage, rosemary and thyme,
Where never sprung water, nor ever rain fell,
  For she once was a true love of mine.

Ask her to dry it on yonder thorn,
  Parsley, sage, rosemary and thyme,
Which never bore blossom since Adam was born,
  For she once was a true love of mine.

Don't-care

Don't-care didn't care,
Don't-care was wild.
Don't-care stole plum and pear
Like any beggar's child.

Don't-care was made to care,
Don't-care was hung.
Don't-care was put in a pot
And boiled till he was done.

Pigs!

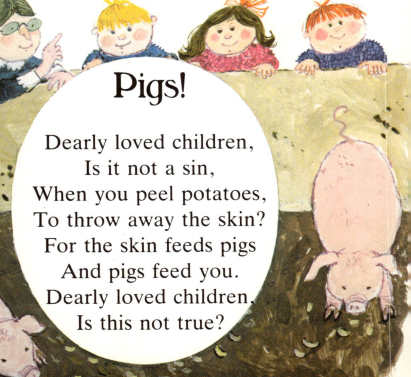

Dearly loved children,
Is it not a sin,
When you peel potatoes,
To throw away the skin?
For the skin feeds pigs
And pigs feed you.
Dearly loved children,
Is this not true?

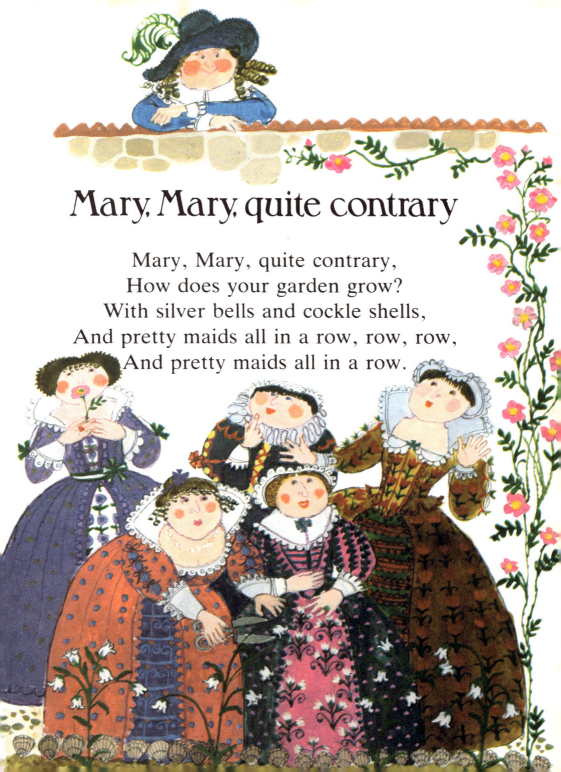

Mary, Mary, quite contrary

Mary, Mary, quite contrary,
How does your garden grow?
With silver bells and cockle shells,
And pretty maids all in a row, row, row,
And pretty maids all in a row.

I saw a ship a-sailing

I saw a ship a-sailing,
   A-sailing on the sea,
And it was fully laden
   With pretty things for me.

There were sweeties in the cabin,
   And apples in the hold.
The sails were made of silk
   And the masts were made of gold.

The four and twenty sailors,
   That ran along the decks,
Were four and twenty white mice
   With chains about their necks.

The captain was a duck,
   With stripes all down his back,
And when the ship began to move,
   The Captain said, 'Quack, quack!'

Monday's child

Monday's child is fair of face,
   Tuesday's child is full of grace,
Wednesday's child is full of woe,
   Thursday's child has far to go,
Friday's child is loving and giving,
   Saturday's child works hard for a living,
And the child that is born on the Sabbath day
   Is bonny and bright, and good and gay.

The house that Jack built

This is the house
That Jack built.

This is the malt
That lay in the house
That Jack built.

This is the rat
That ate the malt
That lay in the house
That Jack built.

This is the cat
That killed the rat
That ate the malt
That lay in the house
That Jack built.

This is the dog
That chased the cat
That killed the rat
That ate the malt
That lay in the house
That Jack built.

This is the cow with the crumpled horn
That tossed the dog
That chased the cat
That killed the rat
That ate the malt
That lay in the house
That Jack built.

This is the maiden all forlorn
That milked the cow with the crumpled horn
That tossed the dog
That chased the cat
That killed the rat
That ate the malt
That lay in the house
That Jack built.

This is the man all tattered and torn
That kissed the maiden all forlorn
That milked the cow with the crumpled horn
That tossed the dog
That chased the cat
That killed the rat
That ate the malt
That lay in the house
That Jack built.

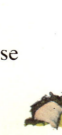

This is the priest all shaven and shorn
That married the man all tattered and torn
That kissed the maiden all forlorn
That milked the cow with the crumpled horn
That tossed the dog
That chased the cat
That killed the rat
That ate the malt
That lay in the house
That Jack built.

This is the cock that crowed in the morn
That waked the priest all shaven and shorn
That married the man all tattered and torn
That kissed the maiden all forlorn
That milked the cow with the crumpled horn
That tossed the dog
That chased the cat
That killed the rat
That ate the malt
That lay in the house
That Jack built.

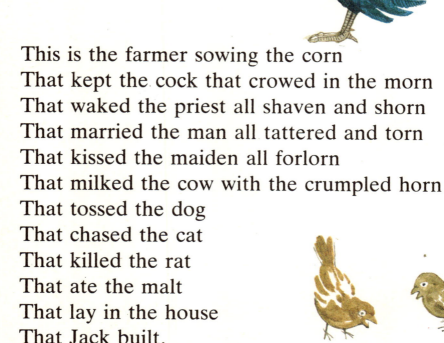

This is the farmer sowing the corn
That kept the cock that crowed in the morn
That waked the priest all shaven and shorn
That married the man all tattered and torn
That kissed the maiden all forlorn
That milked the cow with the crumpled horn
That tossed the dog
That chased the cat
That killed the rat
That ate the malt
That lay in the house
That Jack built.

131

One day I saw

One day I saw a big brown cow
    Raise her head and chew.
I said, 'Good morning, Mrs Cow,'
    But all she said was, 'Moo!'

One day I saw a woolly lamb,
    I followed it quite far.
I said, 'Good morning, little lamb,'
    But all it said was, 'Baa!'

One day I saw a dappled horse,
    Cropping in the hay.
I said, 'Good morning, Mr Horse,'
    But all he said was, 'Neigh!'

One day I saw a tabby cat,
    Walking through the dew.
I said, 'Good morning, tabby cat,'
    But all she said was, 'Mew!'

One day I saw a pretty bird,
   Which fluttered at my feet.
I said, 'Good morning, little bird,'
   But all he said was, 'Tweet!'

One day I saw a greedy pig,
   With mud all done his front.
I said, 'Good morning, Mr Pig,'
   But all he said was, 'Grunt!'

One day I saw a friendly duck,
   With feathers on her back.
I said, 'Good morning, Mrs Duck,'
   But all she said was, 'Quack!'

One day I saw a field mouse
   And thought that he would speak.
I said, 'Good morning, tiny mouse,'
   But all he said was, 'Squeak!'

The old woman
who lived in a shoe

There was an old woman
Who lived in a shoe.
She had so many children
She didn't know what to do!
So she gave them some broth,
Without any bread,
And kissed them all quickly,
And put them to bed.

If

If all the seas were one sea,
What a great sea that would be!
If all the trees were one tree,
What a great tree that would be!

If all the axes were one axe,
What a great axe that would be!
And if all the men were one man,
What a great man that would be!

And if the great man took the great axe
And cut down the great tree
And let it fall into the great sea
What a great splash that would be!

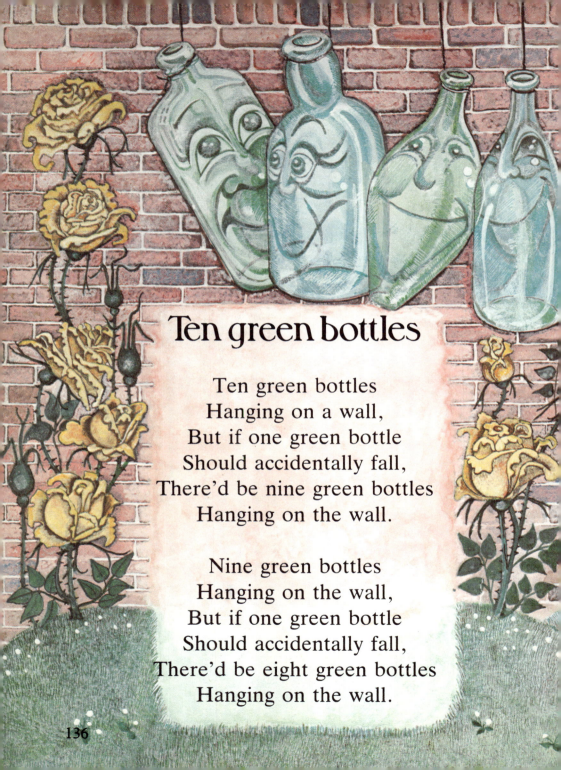

Ten green bottles

Ten green bottles
Hanging on a wall,
But if one green bottle
Should accidentally fall,
There'd be nine green bottles
Hanging on the wall.

Nine green bottles
Hanging on the wall,
But if one green bottle
Should accidentally fall,
There'd be eight green bottles
Hanging on the wall.

Eight green bottles
Hanging on the wall,
But if one green bottle
Should accidentally fall,
There'd be seven green bottles
Hanging on the wall.

Seven green bottles
Hanging on the wall,
But if one green bottle
Should accidentally fall,
There'd be six green bottles
Hanging on the wall.

Six green bottles
Hanging on the wall,
But if one green bottle
Should accidentally fall,
There'd be five green bottles
Hanging on the wall.

Five green bottles
Hanging on the wall,
But if one green bottle
Should accidentally fall,
There'd be four green bottles
Hanging on the wall.

Four green bottles
Hanging on the wall,
But if one green bottle
Should accidentally fall,
There'd be three green bottles
Hanging on the wall.

Three green bottles
Hanging on the wall,
But if one green bottle
Should accidentally fall,
There'd be two green bottles
Hanging on the wall.

Two green bottles
Hanging on the wall,
But if one green bottle
Should accidentally fall,
There'd be one green bottle
Hanging on the wall.

One green bottle
Hanging on the wall,
But if one green bottle
Should accidentally fall,
There'd be no green bottles
Hanging on the wall.

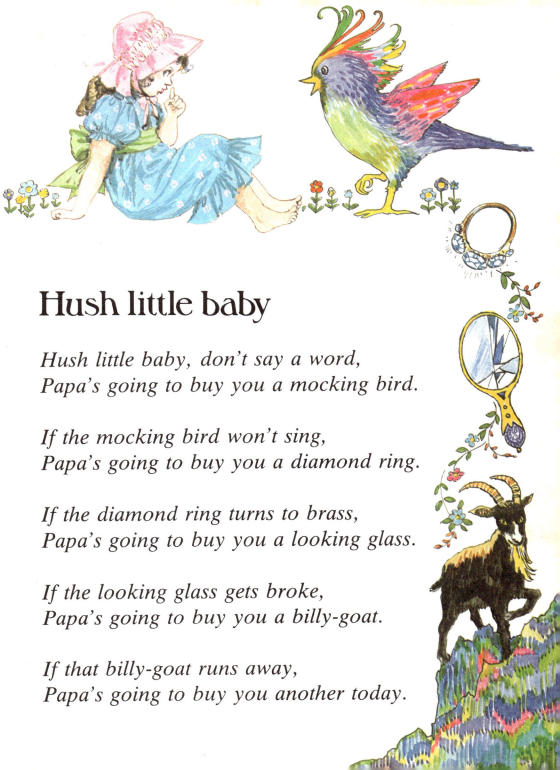

Hush little baby

Hush little baby, don't say a word,
Papa's going to buy you a mocking bird.

If the mocking bird won't sing,
Papa's going to buy you a diamond ring.

If the diamond ring turns to brass,
Papa's going to buy you a looking glass.

If the looking glass gets broke,
Papa's going to buy you a billy-goat.

If that billy-goat runs away,
Papa's going to buy you another today.

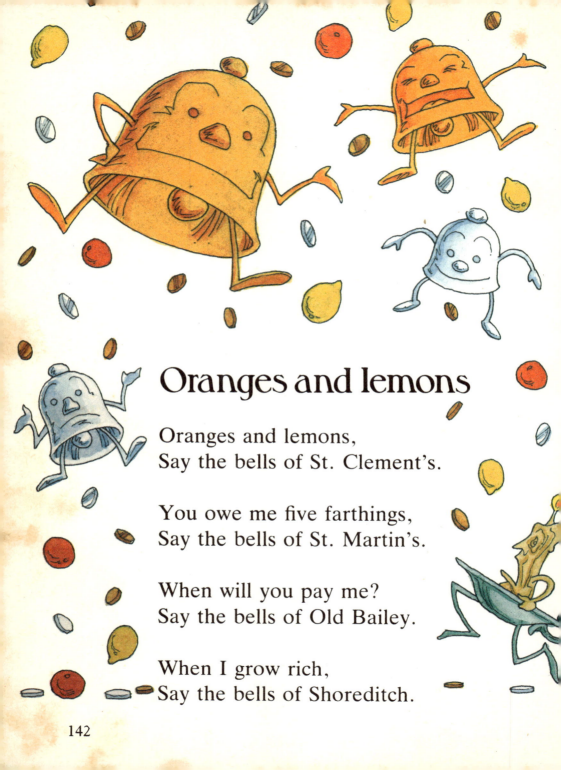

Oranges and lemons

Oranges and lemons,
Say the bells of St. Clement's.

You owe me five farthings,
Say the bells of St. Martin's.

When will you pay me?
Say the bells of Old Bailey.

When I grow rich,
Say the bells of Shoreditch.

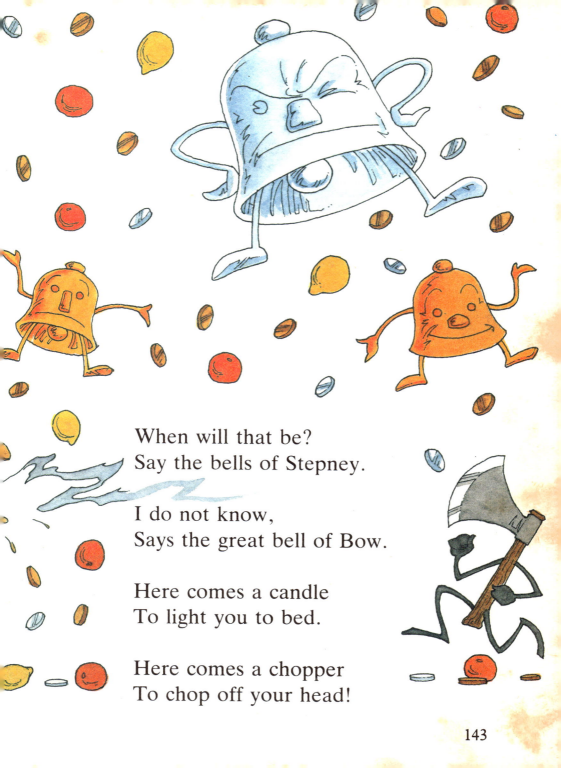

When will that be?
Say the bells of Stepney.

I do not know,
Says the great bell of Bow.

Here comes a candle
To light you to bed.

Here comes a chopper
To chop off your head!

One, two

One, two,
Buckle your shoe.

Three, four,
Knock at the door.

Five, six,
Pick up sticks.

Seven, eight,
Lay them straight.

Nine, ten,
A big fat hen.

144

Eleven, twelve,
Dig and delve.

Thirteen, fourteen,
Maids a-courting.

Fifteen, sixteen,
Maids in the kitchen.

Seventeen, eighteen,
Maids in waiting.

Nineteen, twenty,
My plate's empty.

The alphabet

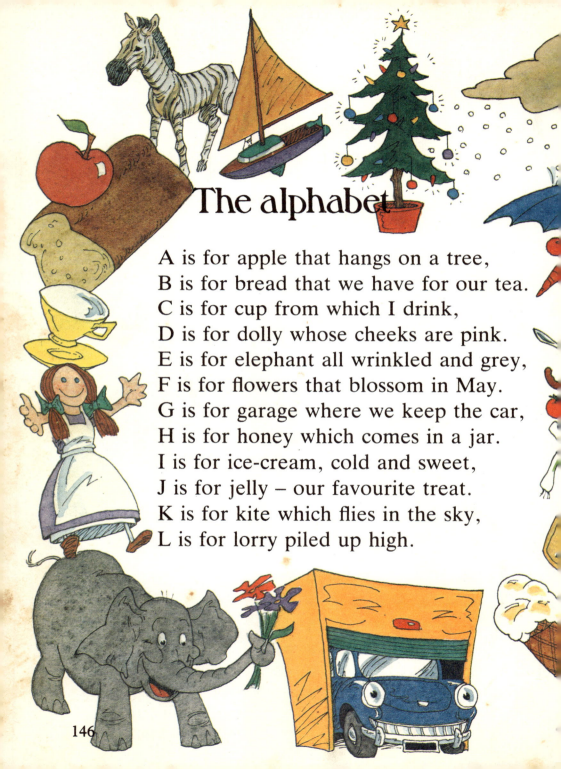

A is for apple that hangs on a tree,
B is for bread that we have for our tea.
C is for cup from which I drink,
D is for dolly whose cheeks are pink.
E is for elephant all wrinkled and grey,
F is for flowers that blossom in May.
G is for garage where we keep the car,
H is for honey which comes in a jar.
I is for ice-cream, cold and sweet,
J is for jelly – our favourite treat.
K is for kite which flies in the sky,
L is for lorry piled up high.

146

M is for milk, all creamy and white,
N is for the note I'm going to write.
O is for orange, round like a ball,
P is for the picture we hang on the wall.
Q is for the queen, who wears a crown,
R is for rain which falls on the ground.
S is for school where we go every day,
T is for toys with which we play.
U is for umbrella which keeps us dry,
V is for vegetables we eat with meat pie.
W is for winter with cold, dark nights,
X is for Xmas tree, glowing with lights.
Y is for yacht I go sailing with you,
Z is for zebra who lives in the zoo.

There were ten in the bed

There were ten in the bed
And the little one said,
'Roll over, roll over!'
So they all rolled over
And one fell out.

There were nine in the bed
And the little one said,
'Roll over, roll over!'
So they all rolled over
And one fell out.

There were eight in the bed
And the little one said,
'Roll over, roll over!'
So they all rolled over
And one fell out.

There were seven in the bed
And the little one said,
'Roll over, roll over!'
So they all rolled over
And one fell out.

There were six in the bed
And the little one said,
'Roll over, roll over!'
So they all rolled over
And one fell out.

There were five in the bed
And the little one said,
'Roll over, roll over!'
So they all rolled over
And one fell out.

There were four in the bed
And the little one said,
'Roll over, roll over!'
So they all rolled over
And one fell out.

There were three in the bed
And the little one said,
'Roll over, roll over!'
So they all rolled over
And one fell out.

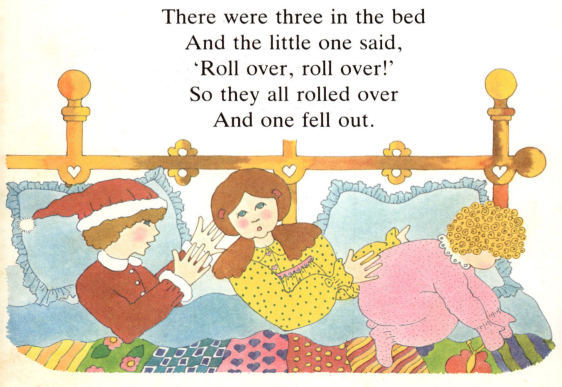

There were two in the bed,
And the little one said,
'Roll over, roll over!'
So they all rolled over
And one fell out.

There was one in the bed
And the little one said,
'Roll over, roll over!'
So he rolled over,
And he fell out.

There was no one in the bed,
So no one said,
'Roll over, roll over!'

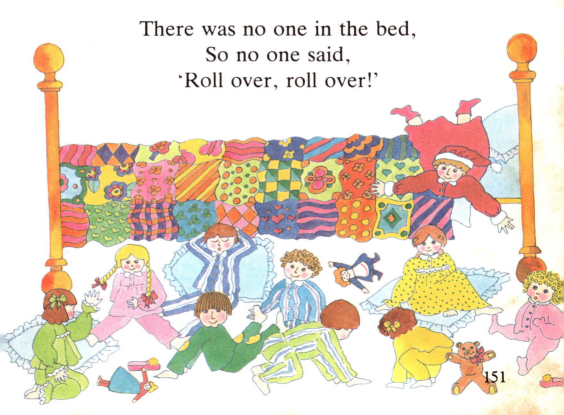

151

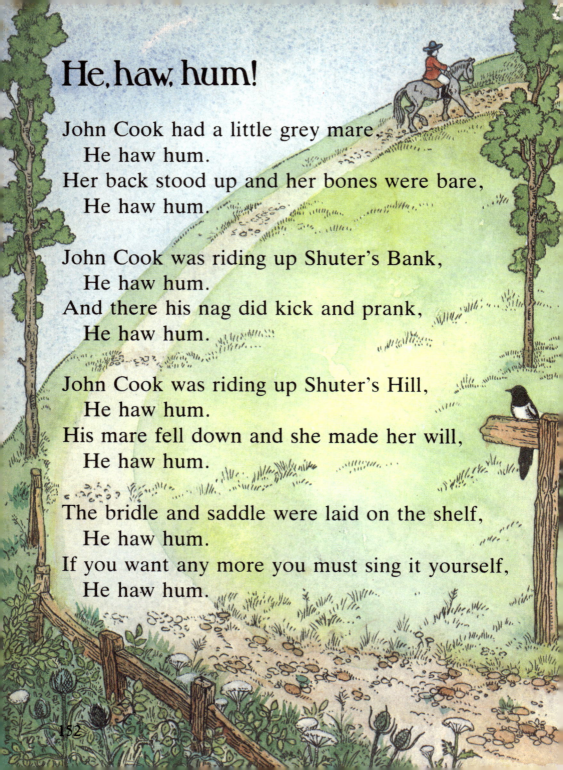

He, haw, hum!

John Cook had a little grey mare,
   He haw hum.
Her back stood up and her bones were bare,
   He haw hum.

John Cook was riding up Shuter's Bank,
   He haw hum.
And there his nag did kick and prank,
   He haw hum.

John Cook was riding up Shuter's Hill,
   He haw hum.
His mare fell down and she made her will,
   He haw hum.

The bridle and saddle were laid on the shelf,
   He haw hum.
If you want any more you must sing it yourself,
   He haw hum.

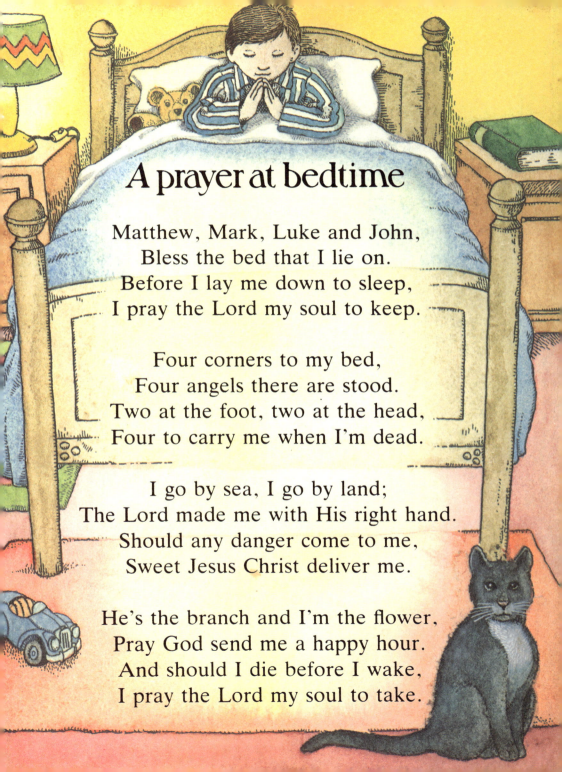

A prayer at bedtime

Matthew, Mark, Luke and John,
Bless the bed that I lie on.
Before I lay me down to sleep,
I pray the Lord my soul to keep.

Four corners to my bed,
Four angels there are stood.
Two at the foot, two at the head,
Four to carry me when I'm dead.

I go by sea, I go by land;
The Lord made me with His right hand.
Should any danger come to me,
Sweet Jesus Christ deliver me.

He's the branch and I'm the flower,
Pray God send me a happy hour.
And should I die before I wake,
I pray the Lord my soul to take.

Index of first lines

155